I Look Like This

by Nick Sharratt

CANDLEWICK PRESS
CAMBRIDGE, MASSACHUSETTS

What do you look like?

I look like this.

When I'm having fun

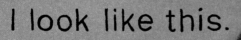
I look like this.

When I'm a
scary monster

I look like this.

When I bang
my thumb

I look
like this.

When Cat is a pest.

And when I'm fast asleep

I look like this.

When I'm ready for bed

I look like this.

When Daddy gives
me ice cream

I look like this.